Walt Disney Pictures

The Black Cauldron

ISBN 0 361 06935 9

Walt Disney Pictures presents
The Black Cauldron
produced in association with Silver Screen Partners II
Based on the Chronicles of Prydain series
by Lloyd Alexander
Music by Elmer Bernstein. Distributed by Buena Vista Distribution Co Inc

Copyright © 1985 Walt Disney Productions
Published 1985 by Purnell Books, Paulton,
Bristol BS18 5LQ, a member of the BPCC group
Phototypeset by Quadraset Limited
Made and printed in Great Britain by
Purnell and Sons (Book Production) Limited, Paulton, Bristol

The kingdom of Prydain was at war, but in Dallben's woodland cottage there was nothing for the boy Taran to do but to mind Hen Wen, the pig.

"Suppose the war's over, before I'm old enough to fight?" he asked Dallben.

The old man was worried. Something was wrong, though he did not know what. He answered the boy testily.

"War is not a game," he said. "Now go and feed Hen Wen."

"Hen Wen—always Hen Wen!" grumbled Taran, but he went to do as he was told. Dallben followed him out.

"She's a special pig, Taran," he began. But he got no further, for just then the pig began to act very strangely, as if something was frightening her.

"Quick, lad, bring her inside!" cried Dallben, running on ahead.

Taran carried Hen Wen into the cottage, and was surprised to see a pail of water on the floor, with lighted candles all around it.

"What's that for?" he asked.

"Put Hen Wen down," said Dallben. "I never use her powers unless I have to—but now I must."

What was Dallben talking about? wondered Taran, as he placed the pig on the floor.

"Taran, what you are about to see you must never reveal to anyone," said Dallben, gravely. Then he turned to Hen Wen, who stood beside the pail of water.

"Hen Wen, from you I do beseech knowledge that lies beyond my reach," he chanted.

Taran listened and watched in silence as Hen Wen responded to the chant by putting her snout into the water. A glowing light shone out, and then an image appeared on the surface of the water.

"Ah—the Horned King!" said Dallben, softly, as the vision became clear.

"Gwythaints, too—searching for something," continued Dallben, as several large birds of prey appeared with the Horned King in the vision. Then a large black cauldron appeared, and Dallben understood.

"He's searching for the Black Cauldron, Taran, with the help of the Gwythaints," explained Dallben. "That awesome weapon has been hidden for centuries, but should the evil Horned King ever find and use it, nothing could stand against him!"

He broke off as something else appeared on the surface of the water. It was the image of Hen Wen herself.

"Enough!" cried Dallben, plunging his staff into the water to end the vision. Hen Wen took her snout out of the water, and came out of her trance.

"I thought I alone knew the secret of Hen Wen's power," said Dallben. "But the Horned King has learned of it. You must take her at once to the hidden cottage at the edge of the forest, and stay there until I come for you."

"I'm not afraid of the Horned King," said Taran, bravely.

Dallben smiled sadly at him.

"Then you are a very foolish lad," he said, kindly. "Untried courage is no match for his evil."

Taran, knowing that Dallben was a wise man, promised to do as he was told and set out with Hen Wen straight away.

"I had no idea that you were so special, Hen Wen," he said to the pig as they made their way through the forest. "I'll protect you. Now where's a good stout stick to use as a sword? Ah yes, here's one . . ."

When he turned round again, the stick in his hand, Hen Wen had vanished.

Taran began to search the forest calling for Hen Wen as he ran. Hearing a noise he took an apple from his tunic, and holding it out in front of him, moved towards the source of the sound.

"Oh, great prince, give Gurgi great crunchings and munchings!" cried a small bouncy creature, leaping out at him and grabbing the apple.

"You hairy little thief!" yelled Taran. "Give that back!" He brandished his stick.

Gurgi began to howl.

"Now look here!" said Taran, suddenly remembering that there were more important things than apples. "Have you seen my pig?"

"Round fat piggy? Curly tail?" said Gurgi.

"That's her! That's Hen Wen!" cried Taran, excitedly.

"Uh no . . . not see piggy!" cried Gurgi. Then, seeing that Taran was disappointed, he changed his mind.

"Yes, Gurgi saw piggy run . . . right through there!"

Taran was just wondering whether to believe this strange creature when he heard Hen Wen squealing, not far away. Running towards the sound he found himself in a clearing, and was just in time to see one of the Horned King's Gwythaints swooping down to snatch her up in its huge talons.

"Hen Wen!" cried Taran, running faster. He dived towards them, and just managed to grab the bird's tail feathers as it flew upwards with Hen Wen. But a second Gwythaint attacked him, making him lose his grip, and he could only run helplessly after the vanishing birds.

When he reached a rocky cliff face, Taran did not hesitate. Fearlessly he climbed it, ignoring the boulders which fell to either side of him.

In the distance, the birds had nearly reached a castle . . . the Horned King's castle.

"Oh no!" breathed Taran, from the top of the cliff. Behind him, Gurgi was looking, too.

"Great Lord," began Gurgi, nervously. "Not go in there—forget the piggy!"

Taran looked at him scornfully, and started out for the castle.

Inside the castle the servants were sleeping. The guards were snoring, too, and did not notice Taran as he crept past them. One watchdog, though, was alert, and its barking wakened the man on watch, who set off with the dog to search the many corridors.

Taran crept away in another direction, and came upon a room full of guards and dancing girls, having a party. Unseen, he hid and watched.

An explosion in the doorway made everyone stop and stare. Through wafting smoke a horned image appeared. Taran had seen it before, in the pail of water in Dallben's cottage, and he froze with terror as he recognised the form of the Horned King.

"Welcome, Your Majesty!" cried a green dwarf, creeping forward. "We were just celebrating our success—I mean, *your* success . . . bring in the prisoner!"

To Taran's horror, Hen Wen was led in, shackled in chains.

"There, Sire," laughed the dwarf, Creeper. "This is the pig that creates visions!"

A pail of water was set before Hen Wen, and her chains removed.

"All right, pig," said Creeper to Hen Wen. "Show His Majesty where the Black Cauldron can be found!"

Hen Wen looked into the water, and then looked away.

The dwarf angrily pushed Hen Wen's head under water. "I'm warning you!" he screamed. One of the others raised an axe.

"No!" cried Taran, racing towards the pig. "Get back!" He grabbed a nearby broom, and swung it towards the henchman's axe.

It was an unequal fight. Taran was soon a prisoner too, facing the Horned King.

"I presume, my boy, that you are the keeper of this oracular pig?" said the Horned King.

"Er—ah—yes, sir," stammered Taran.

"Then instruct her to show me the whereabouts of the Black Cauldron!" ordered the King.

"Oh, Sir, I—I can't, I promised," whispered Taran.

"In that case," said the King, coldly, crushing a goblet to bits as he spoke, "the pig is no use to me!"

The axe rose again.

"No! You can't!" cried Taran. "I'll make her tell you."

"That's better," said the Horned King.

Remembering how Dallben had chanted to Hen Wen, Taran now did the same. An image began to form on the water as Hen Wen went into a trance, her snout in the pail.

But the Horned King was too impatient. He leaned over Taran, and his glowing eyes frightened the boy so much that he jumped backwards.

"Argh!"

Taran had kicked over the pail, splashing the contents into the Horned King's eyes. He screamed, unable to see for a moment, and Taran wasted no time, but grabbed Hen Wen and ran.

"After them!" screamed the green dwarf.

Falling over each other, knocking down everything in their way, the Horned King's servants chased Taran and Hen Wen through the castle. At last Taran had to stop. A parapet was before him, and there was no escape.

"The moat!" he gasped, peering over. There was just enough time to drop Hen Wen over the parapet and into the water before Taran himself was grabbed and thrown into the dungeon.

"I got him, Your Majesty!" crowed the dwarf to the Horned King. "I caught the boy!"

"But you let the pig go, didn't you, Creeper?" snarled the Horned King.

Down in the dungeons, a trapdoor had opened in the floor of Taran's cell. Through it, came a shimmering bauble . . . followed by a pretty girl.

"I hate this place. The rats do jump out at one so," said the girl, dusting herself down. "I'm the Princess Eilonwy. Are you a lord, or a warrior?"

Taran wished desperately that he could say he was, but answered honestly.

"Er . . . no. I'm an . . . assistant pigkeeper," he admitted.

"What a pity," said Eilonwy. "I was hoping for someone who could help me escape. That wicked old king stole me, you know. He was after my magic bauble, in the hope tht it would tell him the where-abouts of some old cauldron."

"That's why he wanted my pig," said Taran. "My pig can tell the future."

Eilonwy looked at him with interest.

"You'd better come with me, then."

Taran followed her through the trapdoor and along a corridor beneath the cells. The bauble danced ahead of them, sometimes swerving to chase a rat, but always coming back. It led them into a burial chamber, where a huge sword rested on a tomb.

''The warrior king who ruled this land long ago was buried here,'' explained Eilonwy, acting as a guide.

Taran lifted up the sword.

''Well, *he's* not going to use it,'' he said, as Eilonwy watched.

Suddenly there was a lot of noise, and a new prisoner was dragged into the dungeons and chained to a wall.

''You're making a horrendous mistake!'' cried the new prisoner. ''I'm not a spy—I'm a bard . . . I sing—I entertain . . . oh, *do* be careful, sir! These are the hands of an artist! I assure you, I had no idea who owned this castle! I just happened to be passing!''

No one answered him.

''I'm Flewddur Fflam, minstrel of minstrels!''

Taran and Eilonwy hid until the henchman had gone away, and then started to untie Flewddur. They had almost freed him when they heard shouting and running footsteps, and realised they had been missed from their cells. They knew they must flee.

''Make haste, make haste!'' cried Flewddur, and then realised that he was still tied by one hand, and would have to struggle to save himself!

Eilonwy sped on, but Taran tripped and dropped his sword. While he searched for it, a guard spotted him, and punched him into the air. It hurt, but as Taran landed he saw the sword and, grabbing it, managed to deflect the blow of the guard's axe as it fell towards him. As he swung the sword, it sparked with magic energy and reduced the axe to smithereens.

"No—no—no!" gasped the guard, cowering away.

At once Taran realised what a wonderful sword he had found. Laughing, he began to wave the sword around, to the amazement of Eilonwy, who ran towards him.

Together they hurried to the drawbridge. Guards came at them from all sides.

"We've got you now!" screamed Creeper, hoping for praise at last from the Horned King.

Time was running out for Taran.

Axeheads smashed into the drawbridge, against which Eilonwy cowered.

"Do something! Use the sword!" she shrieked.

Taran glanced upwards, and saw the chain which held up the portcullis. He swung the sword, and sliced through the chain. Down fell the drawbridge.

"Run!" cried Taran.

Above them the portcullis began to fall . . .

"Stay up—oh please, stay up!" cried Flewddur, racing for the drawbridge. A fierce dog bounded up behind him, and held him back by the seat of his trousers.

Down sliced the portcullis, cutting off the back of Flewddur's trousers. But he didn't care—he was on the draw-bridge, while the dog was behind the portcullis . . .

Out in the forest, Eilonwy mended Flewddur's trousers. But, having regained his trousers, Flewddur found his hat snatched from his head by the excitable Gurgi.

"Gurgi want this!" said the odd little creature.

"Go ahead," gasped Flewddur. Wearing the hat, Gurgi ran off towards Taran.

"Master!" he cried.

"Who's your friend?" asked Flewddur, ruefully.

"He's no friend of mine—he's just a coward," said Taran. "He runs away when there's trouble."

Suddenly Gurgi became very excited.

"Gurgi remember—saw piggy's tracks!" he cried.

It was true. Hen Wen's footprints could be seen clearly nearby, at the edge of a pool.

Following the footprints, Taran, Eilonwy, Flewddur and Gurgi were drawn into the pond and sucked into a whirlpool, landing up in a cave belonging to kind King Eiddileg of the Fairfolk. To Taran's delight, Hen Wen was with them, safe and well; and there was more good news —King Eiddileg could tell them where to find the Black Cauldron.

"If *we* can find it before the Horned King does, and destroy it," said Taran, "we can stop the Horned King."

"It's in the Marshes of Morva," said King Eiddileg. "My servant, Doli, will take you there."

Doli was not pleased at being sent to such a miserable place, but he did as he was told, while King Eiddileg promised to see Hen Wen safely back home at once. The four friends found Morva to be a gloomy, sinister place, and all of them felt rather frightened. Rising from the mist, they saw a cottage, and Taran said they should enter it to look for the cauldron.

Skulls lined the walls, frogs and toads leapt out at them from a trunk on the floor, but then Gurgi gave a shout.

"Behold, Master!"

Taran looked past Gurgi and saw, through a doorway, the silhouette of a cauldron. He ran into the room—but it was full of cauldrons.

Suddenly three witches entered and shrieked angrily at them, threatening to turn them into frogs. It was their cottage, and they were very cross indeed.

Flewddur saved the day, because one of the witches, Orwen, fell in love with him. The minstrel was very embarrassed by this, and frightened too, when Orgoch, another witch, turned him into a frog and threw him into a stewing pot. Orwen changed him back again as he crawled out of the pot, and now Taran wielded his sword to stop the game.

"We've come for the Black Cauldron!" he cried, bravely.

"No one's asked for that in over two thousand years!" laughed the witches. "Can we interest you in a kettle, perhaps? A skillet?"

The sword wrenched itself free and went around the room, slicing through all the utensils hanging there.

"What a sword! I've got to have that!" cried Orddu, the third witch. "We'll trade the cauldron for the sword!"

"You'll not have my sword!" said Taran, snatching it back.

"I'll trade my harp!" cried Flewddur.

"You can have my bauble!" said Eilonwy. But the witches insisted. It was the sword or nothing.

"All right," agreed Taran, reluctantly. The sword immediately vanished. There was a huge explosion, and the cottage disintegrated. A squadron of cauldrons flew overhead. When the mists cleared the Black Cauldron could be seen, outlined against the sky.

They tried to break it up by throwing boulders at it. Even Gurgi tried punching it. In the distance the witches laughed at their futile efforts to break the Black Cauldron.

"It's indestructible," called Orddu.

"The only way its evil powers can be stopped is if a living being climbs into it of his own free will!"

"Gurgi is bold and brave," said Gurgi, at once. "He will climb into the evil cauldron."

He had one foot inside it when the witches continued:

"Of course, the poor creature will never climb out alive!"

Gurgi jumped back again, shaking. The witches, laughing madly, flew away.

While the friends were wondering what to do, the Horned King's guards arrived, with Creeper laughing as he led them forward. Gurgi ran away, but the others were captured, taken to the castle and strung up by their wrists from a high beam. The King's henchmen were busy collecting the dead bodies of soldiers, which the Horned King planned to bring to life.

Taran could do nothing to help himself or his friends as the Horned King arrived, and sneered at them.

They watched in horror as the Horned King threw a body into the Black Cauldron. Instantly they heard the sound of bubbling from the Cauldron, and liquid boiled up and flowed over the side of it. Mist poured out, covering the dead soldiers, and as the mist cleared the bodies came to life again, and started marching, marching . . .

''How horrible!'' cried Eilonwy.

''My Cauldron Born army!'' shouted the Horned King, triumphantly.

''I hadn't planned for it to end like this,'' whispered Taran. Then he felt his hands being untied, and, looking up, he saw that Gurgi was releasing him.

''Gurgi sorry he always runs away when there's trouble,'' said the little creature. ''Now we leave this horrid place.''

But Taran had other ideas. The Horned King had to be stopped— the Cauldron's powers had to be put out of action . . .

''No!'' screamed Eilonwy, as Taran walked forward to throw himself into the Cauldron.

''Gurgi! Get out of my way!'' cried Taran.

But it was too late. Gurgi, whom they had thought to be a coward, had jumped into the Cauldron to save Taran.

The Horned King and Creeper were stunned, and stared in horror as the Cauldron Born army started to crumble away. Slowly the soldiers collapsed into heaps of bones.

''This had better not be your fault!'' cried the Horned King to Creeper, as he ran back towards the Cauldron to find out what was wrong.

Seeing Taran there, he realised at once that he had been outwitted. A desperate fight began between Taran and the Horned King, and they struggled together on the very edge of the Cauldron.

On the Cauldron's surface, the image of the ancient ruler of Prydain, whose magic sword Taran had found, appeared to beckon the Horned King.

"You shall not have me!" screamed the evil ruler, but he was sucked into the white heat of the bubbling Cauldron, which then sank into the ground.

Taran, Flewddur and Eilonwy ran to escape. There was a boat moored in the river beside the castle, so they quickly rowed away. As they did so, they saw the ground where they had stood going up in flames, with buildings and boulders falling everywhere.

Much later, when all was calm, they returned to dry land. Not far away they could see the Black Cauldron floating on the water. Taran was grieving for Gurgi.

"If you've finished with that cauldron, we'll take it," cried the three witches, flying overhead.

"We'll trade it!" cried Flewddur, playing the witches at their own game. "The Cauldron for Gurgi!"

"No, no. We offer you the magnificent warrior's sword."

As she spoke, the sword appeared. Taran looked at it longingly.

"Never," said Taran. "The Cauldron for Gurgi," he repeated.

"It's not possible!" cried Orddu.

"Just as I thought," said Flewddur. "You have no real power, Madam."

The witches were furious. In a flash of intense white heat the Cauldron vanished, and Gurgi's lifeless form appeared beside Taran.

Taran hugged Gurgi sadly, and then, to his surprise, Gurgi hugged him back!

"Come on, Gurgi—let's go home," said Taran, and all four of them began the happy journey home again.